THE WISHING BONE

AND OTHER POEMS

STEPHEN MITCHELL

ILLUSTRATED BY TOM POHRT

CANDLEWICK PRESS
CAMBRIDGE, MASSACHUSETTS

To my father, Nathan Mitchell, M.D., a.k.a.
the Ancient Mariner, who carries my words in his wallet,
and to my mother, Irma Clurman Mitchell, who saved
me (accidentally on purpose) for posterity
S. M.

For baby bear
T. P.

First edition 2003

Library of Congress Cataloging-in-Publication Data

Mitchell, Stephen, 1943–
The wishing bone and other poems / by Stephen Mitchell ;
illustrated by Tom Pohrt. — 1st ed.
p. cm.
ISBN 0-7636-1118-2
1. Children's poetry, American. [1. American poetry.] I. Pohrt, Tom, ill. II. Title.
PS3563.I8235 W57 2002
811'.54 — dc21 2001035062

2 4 6 8 10 9 7 5 3 1

Printed in Italy

This book was typeset in Golden Cockerel ITC.
The illustrations were done in ink and watercolor.

Candlewick Press
2067 Massachusetts Avenue
Cambridge, Massachusetts 02140

visit us at www.candlewick.com

CONTENTS

WHEN I GROW UP

When I grow up and I am wise,
I'll know if needles shut their eyes,
If shadows dance, if worms have knees,
If bears say "Bless you" when they sneeze.

When I grow up and I am old,
I'll know where secret tales are told,
Where dreams are born, where dragons fly,
Where ladders lean against the sky.

And when they think that I am dead,
I'll know who puts the moon to bed,
Who lights the stars, who lifts the sun,
Who leads the planets, one by one.

The Wishing Bone

It happened on a winter's day
(The air was cold, the sky was gray):
Out walking in the woods alone,
I came upon a wishing bone.

I picked it up and wished the sky
As warm and gentle as July.
I wished sweet music in the air
And flowers growing everywhere.

I wished an apple orchard and
A beach with sugar-flavored sand,
A lake, a little birch canoe.
And everything I wished came true.

I wished down tinier than a flea,
Wished up above the tallest tree,
I wished me as a wolf, a shark,
A firefly shining in the dark,

A blade of grass, an ocean wave,

A bear asleep inside its cave.

I wished a talking daffodil.

I wished a dragon I could kill.

I wished a flock of purple geese.

I wished the world eternal peace.

I wished a pair of angel's wings,

And then a thousand other things.

But after many days had passed,

Each wish seemed easier than the last,

And I felt bored as stiff as stone,

And wished the wishing off the bone.

And suddenly I stood at ease
Among the bare and patient trees
One ordinary winter's day.
The air was cold. The sky was gray.

THE TRIAL

"Gentlemen of the jury!" cried
    The prosecuting pig,
As, stepping from behind his desk,
    He danced a little jig.
(Sweat dripped beneath his woolen robes
    And trickled through his wig.)

"The culprit's ears, his eeriness,
    His camouflage, his crime —
All these I shall not talk about;
    I haven't got the time.
The main point to remember is
    That he's a piece of slime.

"Don't bother with the evidence:
    Just scrutinize his face.
His eyes are pools of guilt, his nose
    A tunnel of disgrace.
Weird thoughts stand up inside his brain
    Like flowers in a vase.

"The verdict must be very harsh
  With scoundrels of his ilk.
For Justice is as strong as steel,
  As elegant as silk.
But, I assure you, Mercy is
  A doughnut dipped in milk."

The jury members, waking up,
    Politely clapped their paws,
Though some seemed not to understand
    The gist of their applause.
They'd totally lost track of who
    Had disobeyed what laws.

Which documents had vanished from
    Beneath the iron box?
What money had the kangaroo
    Embezzled from the fox?
And who had bent the hour hands
    On thirty-seven clocks?

In front, as the presiding judge,
    There sat an ancient owl.
Around his shoulders hung a pink-
    And-white designer towel.
"Defense attorney, hurry up!"
    He muttered with a scowl.

"There's been a slight emergency,
Your Honor," said the bear.
"This morning I left all my notes
Stacked neatly on this chair.
But after I returned from lunch
Not one of them was there.

"I know my client's innocent
    But can't remember why.
You'll have to take my word for it:
    He wouldn't hurt a fly.
If only I could find my notes,
    The proof would make you cry.

"However, if you let him off,
　　I'll have you all to tea.
I'll serve you sweets that go beyond
　　Your sweetest fantasy.
Deliciouser than you could dream,
　　And absolutely free.

"I'll serve you muffins, marzipan,
　　And milkshakes for a start,
Then cookies, creampuffs, macaroons,
　　Ten kinds of cherry tart,
A twenty-seven-layer chocolate
　　Whipped-cream-covered heart.

"And last, vanilla ice cream topped
        With mocha-almond fudge.
You'll be so stuffed that it will take
        Two hours till you can budge."
"Not guilty!" cried the jurymen.
        "Not guilty!" cried the judge.

At first the pig was furious,
        Responding with a glare.
But after his fifth apple pie
        And twenty-first eclair,
He came to the conclusion that
        The verdict was quite fair.

THE WHITE RHINOCEROS

I took a number 7 bus
To see the White Rhinoceros.

I rang the bell. He let me in
And said, "Hello. How have you been?"

I told him all my hopes and fears.
He looked at me and flicked his ears.

I told him all my fears and hopes.
He handed me two telescopes.

I questioned him about his horn.
He said, "Before the world was born."

"But how," I asked him, "can that be?"
He said, "And now it's time for tea."

I left his house at half-past-four.
He chuckled as he shut the door.

Perpetual Number Song

1 is singing,
And 2 is sad.
3 is beautiful,
And 4 is bad.

5 is lazy,
And 6 is late.
7 is fast enough
To run past 8.

9 is shouting,
"It's time for 10."
Take the zero off
And start again:

THE SUN AND I

I met the sun out walking
One day in Central Park.
My pocket watch said 9 A.M.,
Although the sky was dark.

I stopped and tipped my hat to him
And leaned upon my cane.
"I hope you are quite well, sir.
It looks like it might rain."

He stood there gazing down at me
(Since he was very tall),
Then said, "For your politeness
I thank you." "Not at all."

"I'd love to stay here chatting,
Amigo," said the sun,
"But really, I must get back home
Before the day is done."

He took a piece of kleenex
(It looked just like a cloud)
And wiped his forehead. "Adios,"
He said to me, then bowed

And walked away. A dog barked,
A bird began to cry.
And I was left there, hat in hand,
Beneath a starry sky.

QUESTIONS

How many inches in a year?
What makes a zero disappear?
And which is older: there or here?

How long must circles spin around?
What stars are in the lost-and-found?
Why can't a mirror make a sound?

What language is the letter Y?
Who taught the hummingbird to fly?
When you are dreaming, where am I?

THE LAST OF THE
PURPLE TIGERS

To Reeve Lindbergh

She lived in deepest India,
    Beside the River J.
The most convenient airport was
    Twelve hundred miles away.
To reach her, we would have to rent
    Four camels in Bombay,

Then ride ahead to Bangalore
    And rent a large raccoon,
A bear, a boar, two buffalos,
    A blue-and-white balloon.
(We left on January first
    And got there late in June.)

We didn't want to capture her:
    We wanted just to look.
We'd read the buzz about her in
    The Total Tiger Book.
(We brought four crates of gumdrops so
    We wouldn't need to cook.)

We knew she was the last one left
    Of all the purple kind —
The very rarest animal
    That you could ever find.
Just three men had set eyes on her
    (And two of them were blind).

But let me introduce our team:
    First, Mr. Milton Muggs.
    He'd made a fortune selling fish
    And oriental rugs
    But was best known for his exhaustive
    Catalogue of bugs.

Professor Mantovanity
    Came second, straight from Rome:
Courageous, handsome, passionate,
    And shorter than a gnome.
He always combed his ears, because
    He had no hair to comb

Third was the great photographer
    Aurelian Q. Zinc,
Who'd filmed a thousand creatures, from
    The mantis to the mink,
Developing each photo as
    He tap-danced in the sink.

And last of all, though not the least
    (Okay . . . I'll take a bow),
Was me: Gerard the Talking Chimp,
    The Toast of Old Macao.
(You didn't think this poem was by
    A monkey — did you now?)

One night we reached the River J
    (Much later than we'd planned).
The four of us, with bated breath,
    Walked forward, hand in hand.
An orange hippopotamus
    Lay sleeping in the sand.

We saw a herd of crimson deer,
    A turquoise porcupine,
Some lavender rhinoceroses —
    Maybe eight or nine —,
A pair of sky-blue cobras coiled
    Beneath a sky-blue vine,

Two dozen golden mongooses
    (Or should I say "mongeese"?)
And thirty-seven pearl-gray lambs
    With lemon-yellow fleece
(Two-thirds of them were skinny and
    The other third obese).

The moon was full, its silver lips
    Were rounded in an O,
As if amazed by everything
    It witnessed down below.
We walked straight forward, single file,
    As fast as we could go.

And there she was: so suddenly
     That none of us dared speak,
Her long, soft, black-striped purple fur
     So beautiful, so chic,
That our four hearts were in our mouths
     And our eight knees were weak.

We stopped. We stared. We stammered out
     "Hello" a dozen ways.
My tongue felt limp as liverwurst.
     My mind was in a daze,
As if it were a slice of bread
     Spread thick with mayonnaise.

"Oh Tiger, Tiger dear," I said,
    "Dear Tiger, burning bright"
(The words were from my favorite poem),
    "It is with much delight
That we at last have found you in
    The forests of the night."

She raised a purple eyebrow. Then
    Her tail began to stir.
That rumbling, grumbling noise — was it
    A growl or a purr?
Would it be best to take our leave
    Or stay just where we were?

All four of us were very scared,
    But I was scared the most.
My hairs together stood up stiff
    As if they'd seen a ghost.
My mind lay flat before me like
    A piece of buttered toast.

I scratched my ears, I scratched my chin:

    What could, what should we do?

I did a dozen somersaults

    But didn't have a clue.

My mind was in a lather, like

    A headful of shampoo.

What was the Tiger thinking? Was
She angry? Was she bored?
I made a hundred faces but
Felt absolutely floored.
And then the Tiger all at once
Leaned back her head and roared

With laughter. We were so relieved,
    We hugged ourselves in glee.
(It helps to have along with you
    The kind of chimpanzee
That tigers find amusing. Yes,
    It helps to have a Me.)

I've told this story many times —
    To all the magazines,
To paupers and to presidents,
    To communists and queens,
To diplomats in formal dress
    And journalists in jeans.

I've told them how we camped for months
    Beside the tiger's lair —
Professor M and Zinc and I
    And Muggs the millionaire.
We hardly let her out of sight;
    We trailed her everywhere.

We watched her by the riverbank,
  We watched her on the plains,
We watched her in the blazing sun
  And in the summer rains,
We watched her silent with the ducks
  Or whooping with the cranes.

And when we weren't watching her,
  We put ourselves at ease
Stretched out beneath the branches of
  The barabumba trees.
(Their fruits taste like vanilla fudge
  Plus Gorgonzola cheese.)

Zinc took five thousand shots of her,
    In every purple pose:
While running, leaping, looking at
    A rabbit or a rose,
While resting, as she washed her face
    Or licked between her toes.

(The photos would have been superb.
    But on the very day
We got there, as we all unpacked,
    Zinc found, to his dismay,
That he had brought no film along:
    He'd left it in L.A.)

The summer slowly ended; we
    Were halfway into fall
With our supply of gumdrops getting
    Dangerously small.
We knew we had to take the first
    Free hippo to Bengal,

Then transfer out to Bangalore.
    We waved a sad goodbye
To our dear tiger. All of us
    Were struggling not to sigh,
Especially Professor M
    And Zinc and Muggs. And I—

Well, I do miss her . . . yes, sometimes
    So much that I could weep.
I think about her every day
    And as I fall asleep
I see her purple smile among
    The lemon-yellow sheep.

Yet somehow I keep wondering if
    She's not the very last.
The future is more flexible,
    More marvelous and vast,
Than we can ever really know.
    (We only know the past.)

What if, in deepest India,
    Beside the River J . . .
What if, in that dark forestland
    So many miles away,
She met another of her kind
    One ordinary day?

Her mate! Her very own! A male
    As beautiful as her!
She gazes at his shining eyes,
    His long, soft, purple fur.
And then she slowly walks to him
    And both begin to purr.

What if? What if? And then, someday,

A little tigeroo,

A tiny purple ball of fluff.

Or maybe even two.

Or three or four. It's possible.

I know it is. Do you?

THE ANSWER

It was a bilgy, bulgy night
Inside the whiffle bog.
The ling-langs howled, obstreperous;
The owls, ambideperous,
Fell both ways through the fog.

I came condensed and dire of heart,
My pockets lined with glue.
I bowed; and stood there grinned-upon,
Aghast that I was pinned upon
A certain point of view.

I asked him why, I asked him whence,
I asked him whither-ho.
I asked him if my gravity
Would lift inside the Cavity
And where the greens would go.

He sat up in his velvet chair,
More silent than a sheep.
Perhaps he was considering
A way around my diddering;
Perhaps he was asleep.

I heard the owls go hooling past
The ling-langs' drizzling drone.
I heard the hippos' trumpetsound,
And camels with their crumpetsound
Together or alone.

"Wake up," I called, "salubrious sir."
"Wake up! Wake up!" he said.
And straighter than a chalkingstick,
He grabbed his rubber walkingstick
And hit me on the head.

A light went on inside my brain:
"Aha!" I cried with glee.
The world was bright and boisterous,
And I—released, rejoisterous—
Felt rounder than a pea.

And ever since that bulgy night
Inside the whiffle bog,
I've lived my days in clarity,
My evenings in hilarity,
As fragrant as a frog.